Clare Bevan

Lucky Numbers

Illustrated by David Pattison

HODDER
Wayland

an imprint of Hodder Children's Books

Chapter One

When the final number bounced across the television screen, everyone stayed remarkably calm. Maddie carried on reading her comic. Tom rolled on the floor with Horace the dog. The baby sucked a spoon. Mum stitched the ears on one more toy monkey and added it to the pile she had finished already.

"That makes fifty," she said. "You two can drop them round to Mr Jarvis before supper."

Dad didn't make a sound. He just gazed at the flashing screen and let the announcer's voice wash over him.

"Because last week was a roll-over, this week's jackpot stands at almost twenty million pounds." The crowd went wild. The smiling face continued, "According to our computer there is only one winner, but as yet we have no further details."

"I don't think I'd like to be rich," said
Maddie, flipping to the puzzle page. "But
I wouldn't mind a new bell for my bike.
The old one's so rusty it sounds like
a dying donkey."

"We'd like lots of money, wouldn't we,
Horace?" murmured Tom, scratching the
dog's floppy ears. "We'd spend it all on
food. Loads of bones and chocolate
biscuits for you, and a lifetime's supply
of pineapple pizzas for me. And a pair
of roller blades."

Horace opened one eye and whimpered. He wasn't too sure about the roller blades.

"Well, I'd say goodbye to cuddly toys," said Mum. "And I'd say one or two things to Mr Jarvis while I was at it. He's been swindling me for years. No one else would work all hours of the day and night for the peanuts he pays me."

Dad still didn't speak. His mouth was moving but no sounds came out. No one noticed that his face had gone a funny colour.

"Come on, Horace," said Tom. "Walkies." And he helped Mum load the monkeys into the baby's battered pram while Maddie fetched the lead and the wellingtons.

"Stop," Dad was whispering in a strangled croak. "You don't need to get wet…"

The door slammed. The children had gone. The baby gave a little sigh and sucked its bib.

"Come on, Keith," shouted Mum from the kitchen. "I'm not washing up all these disgusting dishes on my own."

And before he could wring out the words, "I'll buy you a dishwasher," she had thrown a wet tea-towel over his head.

Chapter Two

Nobody in the Carter family took dreams
too seriously. Prizes and golden tickets
were for other people. Even when their
name came out of the hat in the school
raffle, they went home with a tin of sugar-
free prunes instead of the video recorder.
Let's face it, if they had a fairy godmother
she would be the one who failed her final
Wand Exams.

Other families might watch the Lottery programme with their numbers at the ready and their hearts full of hope, but not the Carters. "If we picked the winning combination," said Maddie cheerfully, "I bet that would be the week when Dad forgot to fill in the form. Or three thousand other people would share the money and we'd end up with a cheque for two pounds fifty."

It wasn't until the children came home, damp and depressed with an empty pram and a soggy dog, that Dad managed to speak. "Cheer up," he said. "This could be our lucky day."

Tom snorted. "Try telling that to Mum. Old Jarvis only paid us half-rates, just because a bit of rain dripped on the monkeys and soaked into their squeakers. So now we'll have to make do with baked beans for supper again. Doesn't sound much like a lucky day to me."

"Nor me," agreed Maddie, mopping the worst of the mud off the hall floor. "My boots are leaking. And someone's chewed the buttons off my mac."

Horace whined guiltily and padded off to the kitchen to lick his food bowl. It was already shiny clean but he couldn't help hoping he might find a blob of dried gravy under the rim.

Dad grabbed a chair, thumped it down in the middle of the hall and stood on the seat. "Listen!" he shouted. "It's happened. I mean, it's US. We've scored the goal, we've hit the bull's-eye, we've potted the black."

"What's up with Dad?" asked Maddie, emptying rain water out of her boots.

"Dunno," said Tom.

"He's making a mess on my nice clean chair, that's what," grumbled Mum, shaking her dishcloth at him.

Dad ducked and tried again. "We're rich," he announced. "We're not just rich. We're ridiculously, unbelievably rich. We're rolling in it. We've won the jackpot!" And he waved a slip of paper above his head.

The room had gone very quiet. The baby dropped her bib. Even Horace stopped his slurping. Dad slid down from his perch and mopped his face on Mum's dishcloth.

"The jackpot!" whispered Maddie.

"Are you serious, Dad?"

He nodded in slow motion. "Millions," he said. "We'll never need to stitch another toy monkey together as long as we live."

18

Five minutes later Mum smiled.
"Well," she said. "I suppose this calls
for a celebration. Who'd like a nice plate
of baked beans?"

Chapter Three

It wasn't until the television crew arrived that the family truly believed. Even then they carried on as normal for a whole week, still expecting the dream to end in a puff of grey smoke.

But it didn't. Rosie Red, the presenter of "Bouncy Breakfast Time", interviewed them round her giant toaster, and asked them how their winnings would change their lives.

"Not at all," said Dad, who had already booked a trip to Florida.

"Completely," said Mum, who had still not decided what to do with her heaps of unmade monkeys.

"We're going to put most of the money in the bank," said Tom, who was planning to spend his share on a pizza factory.

"I expect we'll buy a few little treats," said Maddie, who couldn't think of anything she wanted, apart from a new bell for her bike.

"Arf," said Horace, who was beginning to put on weight.

The baby sucked a piece of toast.

For a few weeks their faces were always beaming out from the front pages of newspapers and women's magazines. The telephone hardly stopped ringing, and the journey to school was like a game of hide-and-seek with the reporters.

"All my friends keep telling me what they want for Christmas," complained Tom. "No one ever has a good fight with me any more."

"People stare at me in the street," agreed Maddie. "I think they expect me to wear diamonds with my school uniform. And the only person who still talks to me is Lottie Jones. Except she won't ask me back to her house any more. She says it's too scruffy."

Mum loaded the dinner plates into an enormous dishwasher that had arrived one morning. "Nasty great thing," she said, smacking the door shut. "I can't turn round in this kitchen without banging my elbows on bits of machinery. We'll have to move."

"Brilliant," said Tom, cheering up. "Somewhere with a massive garden. And a swimming pool. And a helicopter pad on the roof."

"And a gardener," added Dad from behind his "Money Matters" magazine.

Horace rolled on the new, white rug. The baby gurgled.

Chapter Four

Three weeks later they were living in their dream house.

It had belonged to a film star, and it came complete with a housekeeper, a cook, a gardener, and a general handyman.

"It's not quite perfect," said Tom. "No helicopter yet. But I like the snooker room. And the private cinema. And the gold taps in the bathroom."

Maddie sat on a velvet window seat, gazing across the smooth lawns where Horace was digging holes. "It echoes," she said. "Everywhere. And Lottie won't come to stay. She says she hasn't got anything nice enough to wear."

"Well, it suits me," said Mum, flopping back on a couch the size of a boat and dipping her fingers in a box of coffee creams. "No shopping to do. No washing. No ironing. No cleaning. No cooking. No dirty dishes. Heaven."

Dad basked among the soft curves of his matching couch and flicked the TV controls. "No getting up early for work," he said. "No rushing round all day while the clock ticks your life away. No traffic jams outside the factory gates. No bills waiting for me on the kitchen table. No worries. Bliss."

Florida was wonderful too, although Horace had to miss it of course. Maddie sent him a postcard to cheer him up.

She didn't write to Lottie. It didn't seem a very good idea, somehow. Lottie's mum couldn't even afford a week at the seaside this year.

Coming home to a strange house was peculiar. The housekeeper welcomed them all in, the cook sent up a tray of tiny sandwiches for weary travellers, and the gardener had filled the hall with fresh flowers.

"But it's like being a visitor in your own home," Maddie whispered to Horace. "My room keeps tidying itself when I'm not looking, and I don't recognize half the clothes in my wardrobe these days."

"Have you tried on your new school uniforms?" asked Mum brightly. "Ever so smart they are. With nice little straw boaters for the summer. You'll love Lushington Hall. The teachers are all dreadfully clever, and you can come home every other weekend. If you want to."

"But I don't want to go away to school," protested Maddie. "I like the old place."

"Nonsense," said Dad. "You don't fit in any more. You said so yourself. You need to be with your own kind."

My own kind, thought Maddie. What's that?

She opened her photo album. There was a picture of herself and Lottie, dressed up in their scarecrow costumes for the village fête. They were both smiling, but her friend's face seemed to have faded already.

Chapter Five

When the children had gone, Mum and Dad leaned back in their couches.

"No mess, no noise – luxury," said Dad, admiring the ceiling.

"No socks to mend, no lunch-boxes to pack – lovely," said Mum, handing the baby to the charming young nanny.

Horace wandered outside and stared sadly at the smooth, silent lawn.

The weeks went by. Christmas drew closer. The children sent letters home.

I want a proper camcorder, and a gold watch, and a professional cricket bat like the ones they use at Lords, wrote Tom, but his heart wasn't in it. The thought of a bulging stocking didn't seem half as thrilling as usual. "Whatever I want, I can have," he told himself gloomily. "Where's the fun in that?"

How is Horace? wrote Maddie. *Can the baby walk yet? It's nice here, but I miss you and Lottie and Mum's rice pudding. Please can we all have silly presents on Christmas morning, like we used to in the old days? Packets of jelly babies and magic tricks and whoopee cushions?*

She lay back on her bed in the dormitory and tried to remember the sound of Lottie's voice. It had been deep and gurgly, as if she was always on the edge of laughter. The girls here just seemed to squeak like toy monkeys.

Chapter Six

Christmas was amazing. There was no doubt about that. A colossal tree brushed the ceiling with a genuine silver star and there were enough parcels to fill a whole department store. Cook produced a pudding the size of a watermelon. Horace ate smoked salmon, venison, gift-wrapped bones and a boxful of luxury choc drops.

He was also very sick.

That evening the family sat before their Cinemascope TV screen. There wasn't much else to do. None of their friends had wanted to pop in for party games or supper.

"Here is the latest report from the war zone," said the announcer, removing her "News at Noel" party hat.

Maddie watched the blank eyes of the homeless children and felt the weight of her Christmas presents crushing down on her shoulders. She reached out and took the controller from Dad's hand.

When the screen went blank she looked at the blur of faces. No one seemed particularly happy.

"I hate being rich," she said. "It's lonely. And its boring. I want to go home."

"Well, now you come to mention it," said Mum, "I didn't enjoy my dinner one bit. It tasted delicious, of course, but it's just not the same if you don't cook it yourself. And I can't even cuddle the baby because Nanny says she must stick to her routine."

40

"All I do is stare at the wall," said Dad. "I mean, it's a very nice wall. And I like not having to get up early, but there's nothing to do all day. Even the garden takes care of itself. I feel totally useless."

Tom fingered his gold watch. "It was great at first," he said. "But I don't really like cricket. Or fencing. Or wearing a bow-tie all the time. I want to play roller-hockey with the gang again."

Horace panted hopefully and rolled off his personal couch. Far away, in the nursery, the baby began to cry.

Chapter Seven

So the big house was sold and the Carters moved back to the village. This time there was a long, straggling garden with plenty of weeds to keep Dad busy, and a comfortable kitchen for family meals. Also a spare room crammed with junk from the glory days. White rugs and smart blazers and unused cricket bats.

Lottie often came round for tea, and nobody mentioned the fact that she wasn't wearing second-hand clothes these days. Or that her mother had booked a proper holiday in a real hotel this summer. The money must have come from somewhere, but Lottie didn't need to ask and Maddie didn't need to explain. There was far too much catching up to do.

Dad gave up reading his "Money Matters" magazine, although he still bought a few tickets for the school raffle every year. Not that he ever won anything. "Luck is a bit like lightning," he used to say cheerfully, "it never strikes twice in the same place."

Mum cooked magnificent puddings, Horace and Tom were their old, scruffy selves and the baby took her first steps.

So what about the jackpot? All those millions? Nobody would say, but I can tell you this much. Someone posted an enormous cheque to a charity for homeless children. Someone sent the local school a lorry full of new computers. Someone bought the cuddly toy company from Mr Jarvis, and made sure that all the workers were paid fair wages.

As for Maddie, whenever she was alone or thought no one could see her, she would smile secretly, like a fairy godmother who has passed her final Wand Exams. Then, just because she was so glad to be herself again, she would take out her Lushington straw hat and jump on it until it was only fit to wear at the summer fête.

She and Lottie were going to be the happiest scarecrows in the whole village.

Look out for more exciting titles in the Red Storybook series:

The Shoe-box Millionaire by Clare Bevan
Frankie has had a money-making idea – funerals for small pets.
Soon orders for Frankie's Furry Funerals (all animals must be small
enough to fit in a shoe box) start pouring in. However, something
happens that takes her mind off money-making altogether.

The Twitches' Bathday by Roy Apps
It's Gert and Lil's one hundred and fourteenth birthday. It's also
their *bathday*, the one day of the year when witches are supposed to
have a bath. But the twitches will do *anything* to avoid having a
wash, even it means paying a visit to the Queen ...

Aliens in School by Jeremy Strong
Max thinks this will be the worst school fancy dress party ever –
he hates his Father Christmas outfit. But the school is invaded by
aliens – Gobbs from the planet Gobble intent on gobbling up all
their party food. Max must do something, but what?

The Tall Story by Frieda Hughes
Micky is always telling lies. Great big whopping ones. But when he
goes to stay with his grandmother, everything he lies about comes
true. And not all Micky's tall stories turn out to be exciting,
especially the frogs in his soup, and his strange allergy to soap...

All these books and many more in the Storybook series can be
purchased from your local bookseller. For more information about
Storybooks, write to: *The Sales Department, Macdonald Young Books,
61 Western Road, Hove, East Sussex BN3 1JD.*